LAUGH-OUT-LOUD PUNCHLINES

ROB ELLIOTT

HARPER
An Imprint of HarperCollinsPublishers

Laugh-Out-Loud: Punchlines
Text copyright © 2024 by Robert E. Teigen
Illustrations copyright © 2024 by Adobe Stock
All rights reserved. Manufactured in Crawfordsville, IN,
United States of America.
No part of this book may be used or reproduced in any manner whatsoever without written permission except in the case of brief quotations embodied in critical articles and reviews. For information address HarperCollins Children's Books, a division of HarperCollins Publishers, 195 Broadway, New York, NY 10007.
www.harpercollinschildrens.com

Library of Congress Control Number: 2023948462
ISBN 978-0-06-328775-4

Typography by Julia Feingold
24 25 26 27 28 LBC 5 4 3 2 1
First Edition

To my whole family: I'm always grateful for your unwavering love and boundless support. This book is a testament to the joy and laughter you bring into my life every day.

Punchlines

Q: What do you call a/an _____ wearing
(type of animal)

earplugs?

A: It doesn't matter—it can't hear you anyway!

Q: Why did the _____ quit going
(kind of athlete)

to the gym?

A: It wasn't working out!

Q: Why was the egg afraid to _____?
(verb)

A: He was a little chicken!

Rob Elliott

Knock, knock.

Who's there?

Ada.

Ada who?

Ada a lot of _____ and now I feel sick!
      (type of food)

Q: What has four legs but can't _____?
                                    (verb)

A: A chair.

Q: How does a deer carry its _____?
                                  (noun)

A: In a buck-et.

Punchlines

Q: What did the conductor say to the

_____?
           (type of instrument)

A: "You're in treble!"

Q: Why couldn't the skunk travel to _____?
                                     (place)

A: He didn't have a scent!

Q: What happened when the frog jumped off

the _____?
        (noun)

A: It felt unhoppy!

Rob Elliott

Knock, knock.

Who's there?

Dragon.

Dragon who?

I'm dragon my _____ to the door!
(noun)

Q: What do monsters like with their _____?
(type of dessert)

A: Ice scream!

Punchlines

Q: What do you call a snowman who vacations in _____?
        (place)

A: A puddle.

Q: What did the ocean say to the _____?
                                    (noun)

A: Nothing, it just waved!

Q: Why couldn't the _____ keep going?
                    (type of vehicle)

A: Because it was tired!

Rob Elliott

Q: What do you call a/an _____ vegetable?
(adjective)

A: A grum-pea!

Q: What do you get when you cross a snowman and a/an _____?
(type of jungle animal)

A: Frostbite!

Q: Why was the cook fired from the _____?
(place)

A: He couldn't cut the mustard!

Punchlines

Q: Why did the chicken cross the road?

A: To show the _____ it could be done!
(type of animal)

Q: Why is _____ **hair so noisy?**
(girl's name, possessive)

A: She has bangs!

Knock, knock.

Who's there?

Alpaca.

Alpaca who?

Alpaca _____ **for our picnic.**
(type of food)

Rob Elliott

Q: What does Frosty do when he feels _____?
(adjective)

A: He takes a chill pill.

Q: What does the _____ have to do before it goes on a walk?
(type of dog)

A: It asks its paw!

Q: Why was the frog excited to have the _____ come to visit?
(type of animal)

A: He wanted to show off his new pad!

Punchlines

Knock, knock.

Who's there?

Yeti.

Yeti who?

Yeti or not here I _____!
                    (verb)

Q: Why doesn't the _____ want
                    (type of bird)

   to pay for a vacation?

A: Because it's cheep!

Rob Elliott

Q: Why was the _____ embarrassed?
(type of food)

A: It saw the salad dressing.

Q: How does the _____ get around in the winter?
(type of insect)

A: In a snowmo-beetle.

Q: Why are _____ always happy?
(type of reptile, plural)

A: They eat what bugs them!

Punchlines

Knock, knock.

Who's there?

Pasture.

Pasture who?

I pasture house on the way to the _____.
(place)

Q: Why did the astronaut leave _____?
(place)

A: She needed some space.

Q: What does the _____ use in science class?
(type of bird)

A: Beak-ers.

Rob Elliott

Q: What does the _____ **like**
　　　　　　　　(type of sea creature)

to eat for breakfast?

A: Muf-fins.

Q: What kind of _____ **never stops**
　　　　　　　　(type of insect)

_____**?**
(verb ending in -ing)

A: A grumble bee.

Q: What happened when everybody rushed to

mail their _____ **at the post office?**
　　　　　　(noun)

A: There was a stamp-ede.

Punchlines

Q: Why didn't the chef season the _____?
(type of food)

A: He didn't have thyme for that!

Q: Why did the chemistry teacher stop

_____?
(verb ending with -ing)

A: She never got a reaction!

Cowboy _____: Round up the cattle!
(name)

Round up the cattle! Round up the cattle!

Cowboy _____: I herd you
(different name)

the first time.

Rob Elliott

Q: **Why shouldn't you give the _____ (occupation) a comb if he goes bald?**

A: He'll never part with it!

Q: **What happened when the students were _____ (verb ending in -ing) in anatomy class?**

A: The teacher thought they were humerus!

Q: **Why did the librarian wear _____ (adjective) glasses?**

A: She wanted to make a spectacle of herself!

Punchlines

Knock, knock.

Who's there?

Omelet.

Omelet who?

Omelet _____**than I look!**
           (adjective ending in -er)

Q: What's something you can catch but not _____**?**
                                              (verb)

A: A cold!

Rob Elliott

Q: Why was the nose feeling _____ at school?
(emotion)

A: It kept getting picked on!

Q: Where do fish keep their _____?
(noun)

A: In a reef-case!

Q: Where do science teachers eat their

_____?
(food)

A: At the periodic table!

Punchlines

Q: What did the _____
(type of sea creature)

say every morning?

A: "Seas the day!"

Knock, knock.

Who's there?

Water.

Water who?

Water your favorite _____?
(plural noun)

Rob Elliott

Q: Why did the whale need a/an _____?
(type of instrument)

A: So it could join the orca-stra!

Q: Why didn't the librarian go to the _____?
(place)

A: Because she was already booked!

Q: What is the _____
(type of animal, possessive)
favorite vegetable?

A: Zoo-chini!

Punchlines

Q: Why did the penguin stay away from the _____**?**
(place)

A: It got cold feet!

Q: Why did the _____ **go to school?**
(type of candies)

A: They wanted to become Smarties!

Q: Where do elephants keep their _____**?**
(noun)

A: In their trunks!

Rob Elliott

Knock, knock.

Who's there?

Wood.

Wood who?

Wood you like to _____ **with me?**
 (verb)

Q: How did the _____
 (type of animal)

escape from the zoo?

A: In a hot-air baboon!

Punchlines

Knock, knock.

Who's there?

Bunny.

Bunny who?

Some bunny ate all my _____.
(type of candy)

Q: Why did the _____ break
(vegetable)
up with the corn?

A: It was ear-ritating!

Rob Elliott

Knock, knock.

Who's there?

Weirdo.

Weirdo who?

Weirdo you think they hid the _____?
(noun)

Q: Why did the _____
(type of vehicle)
have excellent handwriting?

A: It had fine motor skills!

Punchlines

Q: How does the _____ pay for its lunch?
(type of sea creature)

A: With current-sea.

Q: How does the _____ give people a call?
(type of reptile)

A: It croco-dials the phone.

Q: Why did the skunk have to stay in bed for _____ hours until it felt better?
(number)

A: It was the doctor's odors.

Rob Elliott

Knock, knock.

Who's there?

Moth.

Moth who?

Moth _____ got slammed in the door!
         (body part)

Q: Why do monkeys like _____?
                         (plural noun)

A: They find them ape-ealing!

Q: What did the _____ say to the mushroom?
                  (vegetable)

A: "You look like a fungi."

Punchlines

Q: **Why couldn't the firefighter buy the _____ he wanted?**
(noun)

A: Because his money had burned a hole in his pocket!

Q: **What did the _____ say to the banana**
(type of fruit)
when they were playing hide-and-seek?

A: "Keep your eyes peeled."

Rob Elliott

Q: How are the _____ **and the**
(type of reptile)

_____ **the same?**
(type of music instrument)

A: They both have scales.

Q: What is as big as the _____
(type of animal)

but weighs zero pounds?

A: The _____ shadow.
(same animal, possessive)

Q: Why did the _____ **go to the library?**
(type of bird)

A: It was looking for bookworms.

Punchlines

Q: What did the dog say when he tried to chew the _____?
                      (noun)

A: "That was ruff!"

Q: What do you get when you cross an elephant with a/an _____?
                      (type of fish)

A: Swimming trunks.

Q: How does the _____ pay its bills?
              (type of sea creature)

A: With sand dollars.

Rob Elliott

Q: **Why is it easy to play tricks on the _____ lollipops?**
(type of fruit)

A: They're suckers!

Q: **What do you do if your _____ steals your spelling homework?**
(kind of dog)

A: Take the words right out of his mouth!

Q: **Why did the _____ go to the store?**
(type of bird)

A: To get a tweet.

Punchlines

Q: Why couldn't the polar bear get along with the _____?
(type of animal)

A: They were polar opposites.

Q: What did the _____
(type of farm animal)
say to the hen?

A: "Don't count your chickens before they hatch."

Q: What did Darth Vader say to his _____?
(type of relative)

A: "You're a Trooper."

Rob Elliott

Q: How do you know if someone ran into your _____?
(noun)
A: Look at the evi-dents.

Q: Why did the squirrels go to dinner and _____?
(fun activity)
A: They were nuts about each other!

Q: What did the pepperoni say to the _____?
(pizza topping)
A: "You have a pizza of my heart!"

Punchlines

Q: Why did the gardener give her boyfriend a/an

_____?
　　　　(type of flower)

A: Because it was a budding romance.

Q: Why do turtles like _____?
　　　　　　　　　　　　　　　(name of holiday)

A: They like to shell-ebrate!

Q: Why can't you invite a chef to your

_____ **party?**
　　　(name of holiday)

A: Because they'll grill you with a lot of questions!

Rob Elliott

Q: Why did the detective fall asleep at the _____?
(place)

A: It was a pillow-case.

Knock, knock.

Who's there?

Seymour.

Seymour who?

If you Seymour _____,
(kind of treats)

share them with me!

Punchlines

Q: What do you call it when a black belt and a/an _____ (type of athlete) fall in love?

A: Martial hearts.

Q: Why can't you give your _____ (kind of pet) the TV remote?

A: It'll keep hitting the paws button.

Q: What did the farmer say to the _____ (type of farm animal)?

A: "It's pasture bedtime!"

Rob Elliott

Q: Why did the fawn put on the _____?
(type of clothing)

A: Because it was buck naked!

Q: What happens when you sing _____
(favorite song)
to a snowbank?

A: It will drift off to sleep!

Q: Why did the baker give everybody a free _____?
(kind of bread)

A: Because he had a lot of dough!

Punchlines

Q: How did the pony break her _____?
(noun)

A: She wouldn't stop horsing around.

Knock, knock.

Who's there?

Funnel.

Funnel who?

The funnel start once the _____
(adjective)

_____ shows up to the party!
(noun)

Rob Elliott

Q: What do boxers like to drink at parties?

A: _____ punch!
  (type of fruit)

Q: What is the best way to keep the _____ from smelling?
  (kind of animal)

A: Hold its nose!

Q: Why won't you ever see the _____ cry?
  (type of dessert)

A: Because he's one tough cookie.

Punchlines

Q: How do you make a strawberry shake?

A: Introduce it to a/an _____.
                          (scary creature)

Q: Why didn't the turkey want _____
                                   (type of dessert)
after Thanksgiving dinner?

A: It was too stuffed.

Q: Why was the _____
                    (animal that jumps)
so happy on February 29?

A: Because it was leap year!

Rob Elliott

Q: Why did the _____ agree to go to the dentist?
(type of animal)

A: It didn't want to hurt its fillings!

Q: Why did the scarecrow win the _____ for a prize?
(noun)

A: Because he was outstanding in his field!

I used to play piano by ear.

But now I use my _____!
(body part)

Punchlines

Q: Why did the bird get in trouble at the _____?
(place)

A: For tweeting people badly!

Knock, knock.

Who's there?

Yukon.

Yukon who?

Yukon have the _____
(kind of treat)
for dessert tonight!

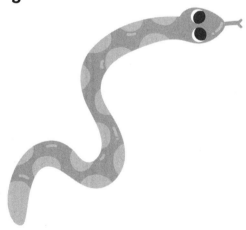

Rob Elliott

Q: What do you call a bunch of cows that live together in _____?
(place)

A: A cow-moonity!

Knock, knock.

Who's there?

Cold.

Cold who?

Cold you come out and play _____
(name of a game)
with me?

Punchlines

Q: What is the best day of the week to take your _____ to the beach?
(noun)

A: Sun-day!

Q: Why did the boy study his book at _____?
(time of day)

A: It was about time!

Q: Why did the vampire take some

_____?
(kind of medicine)

A: He was coffin!

Rob Elliott

Q: Why did the _____ buy a paintbrush?
(type of bird)

A: Because a picture is worth a thousand worms!

Q: Why wouldn't the lobster share its _____ with its friends?
(noun)

A: Because lobsters are shell-fish!

Q: What happened after the _____ got in a fight with a cat?
(type of animal)

A: They hissed and made up!

Punchlines

Knock, knock.

Who's there?

Cannoli.

Cannoli who?

I cannoli eat one more helping of

_____.
(type of food)

Q: Why did _____
(boy's name)
get a boat for Christmas?

A: Because it was on sail!

Rob Elliott

Q: How did the Pilgrims make their _____?
(kind of dessert)

A: With May-flour!

Q: What do you get when a trick-or-treater gives you all her _____?
(type of candies)

A: A blessing in disguise!

Q: Why couldn't the _____ teacher sleep at night?
(type of stringed instrument)

A: Because he was always fretting!

Punchlines

Q: Where do pigs keep their dirty _____?
(type of clothing)

A: In the ham-per.

Q: Where does the _____ keep its car?
(type of dog)

A: In the barking lot.

Q: Which size cup of _____ tastes the best?
(type of beverage)

A: A medi-yum!

Rob Elliott

Q: What did _____ say when
(girl's name)
_____ made her some coffee?
(boy's name)
A: "Thanks a latte!"

Q: What happened when the skeleton built the

_____?
(noun)
A: It worked its fingers to the bone!

Q: What did the archer wear to the _____?
(place)
A: A bow tie.

Punchlines

Q: Why did the _____
(occupation)
fall in love with the baker?

A: She was a cutie pie!

Q: Why did the train engine go to _____?
(place)

A: To blow off some steam!

Q: Why did the snail drink a big cup of

_____?
(type of drink)

A: He was feeling sluggish.

Rob Elliott

Q: Why did _____ fall in love with the sandman?
　　　　　(Disney princess)

A: She thought he was dreamy!

Q: Why did coach call the fire department during the _____ game?
　　　　　　　　　　　　　　　　　　(sport)

A: He was too fired up!

Q: What did _____ call his false teeth?
　　　　　(name of a president)

A: Presi-dentures.

Punchlines

Q: Why did the _____
(type of animal)
break up with the snail?

A: The relationship was moving too slowly.

Knock, knock.

Who's there?

Ice cream.

Ice cream who?

Ice cream if I don't get the _____
(adjective)
_____ for my birthday!
(noun)

Rob Elliott

Q: How does _____ frost their birthday cake?
　　　　　　　(famous singer)

A: With "I sing."

Q: What happened when the farmer fed the _____ food to the _____?
　　　　　　　　　　　　　　　　(type of farm animal)　　　　　　　　　(different farm animal)

A: He felt sheepish!

Q: What do you call a squirrel on _____?
　　　　　　　　　　　　　　　　　　　　(name of planet)

A: An astro-nut!

Punchlines

Q: What do you call a cow that can jump over the _____ in a single bound?
(noun)

A: Legen-dairy!

Q: What do you get when you cross an elephant and a/an _____?
(name of monster)

A: I don't know, but it's gro-tusk!

Q: Why did Santa become an actor in _____?
(movie title)

A: The director thought he had stage presents!

Rob Elliott

Knock, knock.

Who's there?

Olive.

Olive who?

Olive the way you _____!
(verb)

Q: Why did the baker turn down _____ dollars?
(number)

A: He said he had all he kneaded.

Punchlines

Q: Why wouldn't the bicycle _____
(verb)
with its friends?

A: Because it was two-tired.

Q: Why did the math book feel stressed out?

A: Because it had too many _____ problems!
(adjective)

Q: What do you get when a dentist cleans
_____ **teeth?**
(name of monster, possessive)

A: A brush with death!

Rob Elliott

Q: How do you fix a broken _____
(noun)
in the winter?

A: With i-glue.

Q: How do you feel when a giant lizard steps on your _____**?**
(body part)

A: Dino-sore!

Q: How does the _____ **hide in the desert?**
(type of animal)

A: It wears camel-flage.

Punchlines

Q: Why did the bees take a special trip to _____?
(place)

A: Because it was their honeymoon!

Q: Why don't rabbits go on the _____?
(theme park ride)

A: It's too hare-raising!

Q: Why were the bacon and the _____ laughing?
(breakfast food)

A: Because the egg cracked a yoke!

Rob Elliott

Q: What is the _____
(type of bird, possessive)
favorite subject in school?

A: Owl-gebra.

Q: Why did the _____ laugh at the
(forest animal, plural)
owl?

A: They thought he was a hoot!

Q: How is the _____
(school subject)
teacher like a thermometer?

A: They both have degrees.

Punchlines

Q: What did the light bulb say to the _____?
    (noun)
A: "I love you a watt!"

Q: What do you call a scarecrow that always follows you to the _____?
    (place)
A: A corn stalker!

Q: What do you get when you cross a rabbit and a/an _____?
    (type of insect)
A: Bugs Bunny.

Rob Elliott

Q: What's the _____ favorite game show?
(type of sea creature, possessive)

A: *Whale of Fortune*!

Q: Why did the _____ go to medical school?
(type of fish)

A: It wanted to be a sturgeon!

Q: Where do astronauts keep their _____?
(type of food)

A: In their launch box!

Punchlines

Knock, knock.

Who's there?

Axe.

Axe who?

Can I axe you for the _____**?**
                                    (noun)

Q: What did the _____
                              (type of nut)
say to the peanut in a race?

A: "I'm going to cashew!"

Rob Elliott

Q: How do ducks celebrate _____?
(name of holiday)

A: With fire quackers!

Q: What happened to the _____
(type of insect)

when it died?

A: It turned into a zom-bee!

Q: Why did the duck fly south in the _____?
(season)

A: Because it was too far to walk!

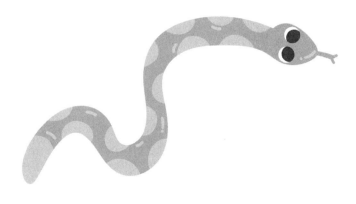

Punchlines

Q: **How did the _____ (type of tree) send its mom an email?**

A: It logged on!

Q: **How does the abominable snowman carry its _____ (noun) ?**

A: In its snowpack!

Q: **Why did the _____ (type of plant) go to the hairstylist?**

A: It wanted to color its roots!

Rob Elliott

Knock, knock.

Who's there?

Muffin.

Muffin who?

I'm muffin without my _____
(adjective)

_____!
(noun)

Q: Why did the boy serve _____
(type of beverage)

on the roof?

A: Because he told everyone the drinks were on the house!

Punchlines

Q: When does _____ cause it to rain?
(type of dessert)

A: When you add sprinkles!

Q: What do you call the _____
(type of animal)
with a rubber toe?

A: Roberto!

Q: What did the _____
(school subject)
teacher say to the pencil?

A: "You're looking sharp today!"

Q: How do you find out the weather on top of _____?
(name of mountain)

A: You climate!

Q: Why didn't _____ (name of girl) laugh at the cattle joke?

A: Because she'd already herd it!

Q: Why did the weight lifter take _____ (book title) to the gym?

A: He wanted it to get ripped!

Punchlines

Q: Where is the worst place to buy a/an

_____?
(type of dog)

A: The flea market!

Q: Why do plumbers like to sing?

A: They have _____ pipes!
              (adjective)

Q: How did the farmer get caught stealing the

_____?
(noun)

A: The pigs squealed on him!

Rob Elliott

Q: Who brings Christmas presents to every _____?
(type of sea creature)

A: Santa Jaws!

Knock, knock.

Who's there?

Norway.

Norway who?

Norway am I buying you the _____ (adjective) **_____ for your birthday!**
(noun)

Punchlines

Q: What did the snowman order _____
(number)

of from the menu?

A: Brrrrrr-itos!

Q: How do you make a/an _____ **shake?**
(type of fruit)

A: Take it to a scary movie!

Q: What do grandfather clocks and

_____ **have in common?**
(type of dog, plural)

A: They both have ticks!

Rob Elliott

Q: Why did the cowboy move _____ (number) cows to New York City?

A: He was de-ranged!

Q: What do you call the _____ (type of dinosaur) that always complains?

A: A whine-osaur!

Q: How do you quit eating Thanksgiving _____ (type of food)?

A: You quit cold turkey!

Punchlines

Q: How did Dracula fight off _____ (number) men at once?

A: It was hand-to-hand com-bat!

Q: Why did the boxer tell _____ (adjective) jokes to everybody?

A: He loves a good punchline!

Q: What do penguins like on their _____ (type of food)?

A: Chilly sauce!

Rob Elliott

Q: What happened when the _____ (body of water) challenged the _____ (body of water) to a race?

A: They tide.

Q: How do horses drink their _____ (type of beverage)?

A: Through a straw!

Punchlines

Q: Why did the clock get detention?

A: Because it tocked too much in

_____ class.
(teacher's name, possessive)

Knock, knock.

Who's there?

Mustache.

Mustache who?

I mustache you to give me some of your

_____.
(noun)

Rob Elliott

Q: Why did the pig buy _____ new dresses?
(number)

A: Because she was so sty-lish.

Q: Why was _____ mad at Santa?
(name of reindeer)

A: He drove him up the wall.

Q: Did Santa pay _____ dollars for his sleigh?
(number)

A: Nope, it was on the house!

Punchlines

Q: Why did the _____ cross the ocean?
 (type of sea creature)

A: To get to the other tide!

Q: Why couldn't the pony sing _____
 (song title)

at the talent show?

A: Because it was a little horse!

Q: What does a trash collector eat after his

_____?
 (favorite dinner food)

A: Junk food.

Rob Elliott

Q: How did the cows pay for their new _____?
(noun)

A: With moo-lah.

Knock, knock.

Who's there?

Reindeer.

Reindeer who?

There's reindeer, so _____
(verb)
home before you get wet!

Punchlines

Q: Why did the farmer order a _____?
(coffee drink)

A: He needed more calf-eine!

Q: Why did the clock go to _____
(place)
for a vacation?

A: It was wound up!

Q: Why did the turkey lose the _____ game?
(sport)

A: He had too many fowls.

Rob Elliott

Q: What do you call someone whose _____ breaks down?
(type of vehicle)

A: A cab.

Knock, knock.

Who's there?

_____.
(type of animal)

_____ who?
(same animal)

No, _____ **says**
(same animal)

"_____." **Owls say "who."**
(that animal's sound)

Punchlines

Q: How do you wake up a chicken for _____**?**
(name of holiday)

A: With an alarm cluck.

Q: When is a _____ **like a frog?**
(type of vehicle)

A: When it's being toad!

Q: Did you hear the story about the _____**?**
(type of animal)

A: It was a wild tail.

Rob Elliott

Q: How do you decide which pie you should make for _____?
(name of holiday)
A: You weigh the pros and pe-cans.

Q: Why did the scarecrows go to _____?
(place)
A: It was a field trip!

Q: Why did the girl stop carving the _____?
(noun)
A: She was a whittle tired.

Punchlines

Q: **What happened when the rabbit ate too many** _____**?**
(type of treats)

A: She was hopped up on sugar.

Q: **Why did the scarecrow go to bed at** _____**?**
(time of day)

A: He was tired and wanted to hit the hay!

Q: **What did the chicken have to do after eating** _____ **donuts?**
(number)

A: Eggs-ercise.

Rob Elliott

Q: What happened when the Little Pig ran away from the _____ (adjective), _____ (adjective) wolf?
A: He pulled a hamstring!

Q: Why was the corn feeling _____ (adjective)?
A: It was the laughing-stalk of the farm.

Q: What happened when the farmer lost all his _____ (type of vegetable) seeds?
A: His hopes and dreams were squashed!

Punchlines

Q: How can I learn more about _____ spiders?
(adjective)

A: Look it up on a web-site.

Q: Why wouldn't _____ walk in the woods?
(name of person)

A: The trees seemed shady.

Rob Elliott

Knock, knock.

Who's there?

Autumn.

Autumn who?

We autumn eat some _____
(adjective)

_____!
(type of food)

Q: What did the _____ **leaf say**
(color)

to the _____ **leaf?**
(different color)

A: "I think I'm falling for you."

Punchlines

Q: **Where did _____**
(Christmas character)
go to vote on Election Day?

A: The North Poll.

Q: **What do you get when a _____**
(large animal)
sits on a pumpkin?

A: Squash!

Q: **Why did the letter _____**
(letter of the alphabet)
go to the salon?

A: It wanted curly-Q's!

Rob Elliott

Q: Why wouldn't the dad buy his son any _____?
(type of bread)

A: He didn't have enough dough.

Q: What did the _____ wear to the graveyard?
(kind of monster)

A: A Halloween cos-tomb!

Q: Why are pretzels more funny than _____?
(type of snack food, plural)

A: They have a twisted sense of humor.

Punchlines

Knock, knock.

Who's there?

Juicy.

Juicy who?

Juicy my _____ _____?
         (adjective)   (noun)

Q: Why did the _____
                     (kind of monster)
trick Dracula out of his lollipops?

A: Because he's a sucker.

Rob Elliott

Q: Did you hear about the _____ (noun) who was hit by lightning?

A: It was shocking!

Q: What do you get when you cross a chicken with a _____ (type of farm animal)?

A: A cow-ard!

Q: What do you get when you cross a sheep, a _____ (type of vehicle), and a swimsuit?

A: A Lamb-bikini!

Punchlines

Q: What did the lumberjack say to the _____?
(occupation)

A: "Axe me no questions, I'll tell you no lies!"

Q: Where is the best place to hear

_____ **at the holidays?**
(name of Christmas song)

A: North Carol-ina.

Q: Why don't stars carry _____
(plural noun)

in their luggage on vacation?

A: Because they're traveling light.

Rob Elliott

Q: Why didn't the moon eat all its _____ for lunch?
(food)

A: Because it was full.

Q: Why did Humpty Dumpty buy a scarf, a rake, and a _____?
(kind of hot drink)

A: Because he wanted to have a great fall!

Q: Why did the doctor take _____ to the hospital?
(book title)

A: To get its appendix removed.

Punchlines

Q: Why won't a _____ go to school?
(type of dog)

A: They don't like arithme-tick.

Q: When does a _____ fly south?
(type of bird)

A: In Flock-tober.

Q: Why did the _____
(kind of stringed instrument)
go to the gym?

A: So it could stay as fit as a fiddle.

Rob Elliott

Q: Why is Santa so good at growing _____?
(type of vegetable)

A: Because he likes to hoe, hoe, hoe.

Q: Why does a _____ (kind of beverage) **always get in trouble?**

A: Because it's not-tea.

Q: Why did _____ (name of girl) **put on boxing gloves before she studied?**

A: Her mom told her to hit the books!

Punchlines

Q: What is big, gray, and wears _____ (adjective) slippers?

A: Cinderelephant!

Q: Why did the clown need a new red _____ (body part)?

A: Because her old one smelled funny.

Q: What's _____ (teacher's name, possessive) favorite drink?

A: Hot chalk-olate!

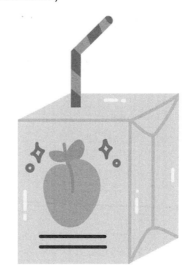

Rob Elliott

Q: What happens if you check out more than _____ books from the library?
(number)

A: You'll overdue it!

Q: Where does a spider go to find the definition of a _____?
(noun)

A: Webster's Dictionary.

Q: How do you throw a party on _____?
(name of planet)

A: You planet!

Punchlines

Q: What does a monkey drink with its _____?
(type of food)

A: Ape juice.

Q: Why was the _____ (type of dinosaur) no longer smelly?

A: It was ex-stinked!

Q: What is the best way to communicate with a _____?
(type of fish)

A: Drop it a line!

Rob Elliott

Q: Why did the _____ **have a stomachache?**
(kind of monster)

A: He was goblin' all the Halloween candy!

Q: What do you call a _____ **that hates Christmas?**
(type of insect)

A: A bah humbug!

Q: Why did the astronaut eat _____ _____?
(number) (type of food)

A: Because he missed launch.

Punchlines

Q: Where does the _____
(type of farm animal)
practice its jokes?

A: The funny farm!

Q: Where do astronauts listen to _____?
(name of singer)

A: On Nep-tune.

Q: How did the frog get over the tall _____?
(noun)

A: It used its tad-pole!

Rob Elliott

Q: What did the baby _____
(type of sea creature)
do when it was lost in the ocean?

A: It whaled!

Knock, knock.

Who's there?

August.

August who?

August of wind blew my _____ away!
(noun)

Punchlines

Q: Why did the lumberjack chop down the

_____**?**
(noun)

A: It was an axe-ident!

Q: What happened when the snail and the

_____ **got in a fight?**
(type of insect)

A: They slugged it out!

Q: Why did the _____ **go camping?**
(type of dog)

A: It wanted to ruff it!

Rob Elliott

Q: What does a frog order at _____**?**
(name of restaurant)

A: Diet croak.

Q: What do _____
(type of vegetable, plural)
do when they see people they don't like?

A: They turnip their noses!

Q: Why are pigs so bad at _____**?**
(sport)

A: They're always hogging the ball.

Punchlines

Q: What has a head and a tail, but no _____?
(name of body part)

A: A penny!

Q: What did the mermaid do when she broke her _____?
(name of body part)

A: She called for a clam-bulance!

Q: Why did the skeleton refuse to go to _____?
(place)

A: He had no-body to go with.

Rob Elliott

Q: What do you get when you cross a _____ **and a firecracker?**
(type of dinosaur)

A: Dino-mite!

Q: Did you hear about the restaurant they put on _____**?**
(name of planet)

A: I hear the food is out of this world!

Q: What is a _____ **favorite sport?**
(type of insect, possessive)

A: Fris-bee!

Punchlines

Q: What did the electrician say to the _____?
(occupation)

A: Let's switch!

Q: How did the farmer fix his _____?
(article of clothing)

A: With a pumpkin patch.

Q: What is a _____
(kind of monster, possessive)
favorite candy bar?

A: Butter-fingers!

Rob Elliott

Q: What do you get when you cross a

_____ **with a drink of water?**
(type of bird)

A: A swallow!

Knock, knock.

Who's there?

Window.

Window who?

Window you want to play

_____ **with me?**
(type of game)

Punchlines

Q: What does a zombie eat with its _____?
(type of food)

A: Mashed pota-toes and grave-y!

Knock, knock.

Who's there?

Alpaca.

Alpaca who?

Alpaca _____ _____
(adjective) (noun)
for our trip!

Rob Elliott

Q: **Which monster can solve _____ (number) math problems in less than a minute?**

A: Frank-Einstein!

Q: **Why was it so windy at the _____ (sport) stadium?**

A: There were hundreds of fans!

Q: **What do you call a really smart _____ (type of insect)?**

A: Brilli-ant!

Punchlines

Q: When do chickens go to the _____?
(place)

A: At ten o'cluck!

Q: How does a barber drive to _____?
(place)

A: He takes shortcuts!

Q: What do bees like on their _____?
(type of dessert)

A: Fro-sting!

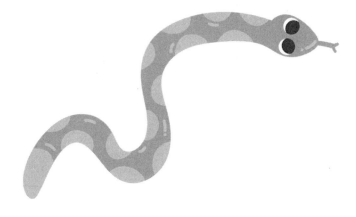

Rob Elliott

Q: **Why did _____ (type of coin, plural) start falling from the sky?**

A: There was a change in the weather!

Q: **What do you get when you cross a _____ (type of vegetable) with a pair of scissors?**

A: Par-snips!

Q: **How did the _____ (type of dinosaur) feel about the first day of school?**

A: It was a nervous Rex!

Punchlines

Q: **What do pigs do at** _____**?**
(time of day)

A: They rise and swine!

Q: **What game did the cows play with the** _____**?**
(type of farm animal)

A: Truth or dairy!

Q: **What do you call** _____ **identical cowboys?**
(number)

A: The clone rangers!

Rob Elliott

Q: What kind of car does a _____
(type of dog)
like to drive?

A: A Land Rover.

Q: What do you call a horse on _____?
(name of planet)

A: A saddle-lite.

Q: What happened after the duck had

_____?
(type of sickness)

A: The doctor gave it a clean bill of health!

Punchlines

Knock, knock.

Who's there?

Justin.

Justin who?

You're Justin time to play _____
(kind of game)
with me!

Q: How did the lizard remodel his

_____?
(room in the house)

A: With rep-tiles.

Rob Elliott

Q: What do lamps wear when they travel to _____?
(place)

A: Shades!

Q: What do you get when you cross a _____ with a propeller?
(type of fruit)

A: A jelly-copter!

Q: How did the banana get out of _____?
(place)

A: It split!

Punchlines

Q: What do you get when you cross a pig with a

_____?
       (type of dinosaur)

A: Jurassic Pork!

Q: Why did the clock read _____
       (number)

books in one day?

A: It had a lot of time on its hands.

Q: Why did the gorilla stop eating

_____?
    (type of food)

A: She lost her ape-tite.

Rob Elliott

Q: Where does a _____
(type of dinosaur)
like to go swimming?

A: At the dino-shore.

Q: What do you call a reindeer who swims in the _____?
(body of water)

A: Ru-dolphin.

Q: What did the light bulb say to the _____?
(noun)

A: "Do you want to go out tonight?"

Punchlines

Q: What did the _____ (type of animal) say when it kissed the porcupine?

A: "Ouch!"

Q: Why wouldn't the jellyfish try out for the _____ (sport) team?

A: He was spineless!

Q: Who gave the mermaid a new _____ (body part)?

A: The plastic sturgeon.

Rob Elliott

Q: **What does a rhinoceros like to eat with its** _____?
(type of food)

A: Horn on the cob.

Q: **Why did the trombone player borrow his friend's** _____?
(type of instrument)

A: His teacher said it's rude to toot your own horn!

Q: **How do crabs buy their** _____?
(nouns)

A: With sand dollars.

Punchlines

Q: What do you get when you cross a trumpet and a _____?
(type of fruit)

A: A tootie fruity!

Q: How did the mermaid call her _____?
(family member)

A: On her shell phone.

Q: How did the orange get into the _____?
(place)

A: It squeezed its way in!

Rob Elliott

Q: Why did the little girl have so many _____?
(type of vegetables)

A: She was a kinder-gardener!

Q: What happened when the _____ (type of fruit) married the _____ (different fruit)?

A: They lived apple-y ever after.

Q: What did the beaver say to the _____ (type of tree)?

A: "It's been nice gnawing you!"

Punchlines

Q: How does a/an _____
(type of sea creature)
get around the busy ocean?

A: It hails a crab!

Q: What happened when the

_____ swallowed the toad?
(type of reptile)

A: It croaked!

Q: Why did the clock go to _____?
(place)

A: It needed to unwind.

Rob Elliott

Q: How do monsters protect their _____ at the beach?
(body part, plural)

A: With sun-scream!

Q: What do you get if your dad gets stuck in the _____ in the winter?
(noun)

A: A Pop-sicle.

Q: What does a/an _____ like to eat while it's camping?
(type of dinosaur)

A: Dino-s'mores!

Punchlines

Q: What kind of exercise should you do after you eat _____?
(type of fast food)

A: Burpees!

Q: What did the banker say to the _____?
(occupation)

A: "You don't make any cents!"

Q: What do llamas have that _____ don't have?
(type of animal, plural)

A: Baby llamas!

Rob Elliott

Q: What did the werewolf do after he was told a/an _____ **joke?**
(adjective)

A: He howled with laughter!

Q: Why did the robber wash his _____**?**
(article of clothing)

A: He wanted to make a clean getaway!

Q: Why did the skeleton drink _____ **cups of milk every day?**
(number)

A: Milk is good for the bones!

Punchlines

Q: What do you get if you cross a/an _____ and a skunk?
(type of insect)

A: A stinker-pillar!

Q: What happens when race-car drivers eat too much _____?
(type of food)

A: They get Indy-gestion!

Q: Why wouldn't the _____ eat the clown?
(type of wild animal)

A: He tasted funny.

Rob Elliott

Q: How can you keep your _____ in suspense?
(family member)

A: I'll tell you later.

Q: Why did the golfer wear two _____?
(article of clothing, plural)

A: In case he got a hole in one!

Q: Why did _____ go to bed with a ruler?
(boy's name)

A: To see how long he slept!

Punchlines

Q: **Where do farmers stay when they travel to** _____?
     (place)

A: At a hoe-tel!

Q: **What did the tree say to the** _____?
                                    (type of flower)

A: "I'm rooting for you!"

Q: **What did the earthquake say to the** _____?
                                           (type of weather)

A: "Don't look at me, it's not my fault!"

Rob Elliott

Q: Why do hamburgers taste best on

_____?
(name of planet)

A: Because they're meteor!

Q: What do cowboys like on their

_____?
(type of food)

A: Ranch dressing!

Q: Why did the pilot paint her jet

_____?
(color)

A: She thought it was too plane.

Punchlines

Q: What happened when the spider got a new

_____?
(type of vehicle)

A: It took it for a spin!

Q: What's more annoying than a cat meowing outside your window?

A: _____ cats meowing outside your window!
(number)

Q: What's the difference between a fly and a/an

_____?
(type of bird)

A: A/an _____ can fly, but a fly can't _____.
(same bird) (same bird)

Rob Elliott

Q: Why do skunks and _____
(type of animal, plural)
always get along?

A: Because great minds stink alike!

Q: Where did the cat buy its _____?
(kind of toy)

A: From a cat-alog!

Q: What did the _____
(type of flower)
say to the bee?

A: "Buzz off!"

Punchlines

Q: Which has more courage, a rock or a

_____?
(noun)

A: A rock—it's boulder!

Q: What happened when the kid's _____ (kind of instrument)

was run over by the school bus?

A: It B flat!

Q: What sometimes runs but never

_____?
(verb ending in -s or -es)

A: Your nose!

Rob Elliott

Patient: I broke my _____ (body part) in two places. What should I do?

Doctor: Don't go to those two places anymore!

Q: Why did the boy eat his _____ (school subject) homework?

A: His teacher said it would be a piece of cake!

Q: Why do pigs like playing _____ (sport or game)?

A: Because they're good at going hog wild!

Punchlines

Q: **Why was the _____**
(type of food)
pretending to be a noodle?

A: It was an impasta!

Q: **Why shouldn't you live on just**
_____?
(type of vegetable, plural)

A: It would be a miss-steak!

Rob Elliott

Q: How does the _____ (type of instrument) player keep his teeth clean?

A: With a tuba toothpaste!

Q: Why did the _____ (type of animal) eat a lamp?

A: It wanted a light snack!

Q: Why wouldn't the hockey player buy a new _____ (noun)?

A: Because he was a cheap-skate!

Punchlines

Q: What do you call a _____
(kind of bear)
with no socks?

A: Bear-foot!

Q: Where do ducks live in _____**?**
(name of city)

A: In pond-ominiums!

Q: Why can't you invite a pig to your _____ **party?**
(kind of holiday)

A: It'll go hog wild!

Rob Elliott

Q: What has _____ feet and sings?
(even number)

A: A choir!

Q: What do you get when you cross a

_____ and a river?
(body of water)

A: You get wet feet!

Q: What is more amazing than a

_____ cat?
(verb ending in -ing)

A: A spelling bee!

Punchlines

Q: What did the forest ranger say to the

_____?
(occupation)

A: "Take a hike!"

Q: Why can't you trust a _____?
(type of vehicle)

A: It'll take you for a ride!

Q: How do you know if there's a

_____ in your refrigerator?
(type of large animal)

A: The door won't close!

Q: What kind of weather only lasts for

_____ seconds?
(number)

A: A hurry-cane!

Q: Why did the sailor buy a boat on

_____?
(day of the year)

A: That's when it went on sail!

Q: How did the baseball player get rid of his

_____?
(noun)

A: He pitched it!

Punchlines

Q: Why don't _____ **sing karaoke?**
(type of bear, plural)

A: It's too em-bear-assing!

Q: How does an alligator make its

_____**?**
(type of food)

A: In a croc-pot!

Q: Where does the _____
(type of fruit)

take a nap?

A: On an apri-cot.

Rob Elliott

Knock, knock.

Who's there?

Diesel.

Diesel who?

Diesel be a great day to wash my _____ .
(noun)

Q: Where does a _____
(type of reptile)
 keep his milk?

A: In the refriger-gator.

Punchlines

Q: What do you get when you throw the

_____ in the snow?
　　　(type of vegetable)

A: Cold slaw.

Q: How does the _____
　　　　　　　　　　　　(type of dog)

celebrate its birthday?

A: With pup-cakes!

Q: What do you get when you cross a/an

_____ and an ear of corn?
　　(type of insect)

A: Cobwebs!

Rob Elliott

Q: Where do you mail your _____?
(article of clothing)

A: To your home ad-dress.

Q: What does the _____ drink at the gym?
(type of reptile)

A: Gator-ade.

Q: What happened when the man stole a blanket from his _____?
(relative)

A: He had a quilt-y conscience!

Punchlines

Q: Why is _____
(name of teacher)
in charge everywhere they go?

A: They control all the rulers.

Q: Where do _____
(color)
crayons go for spring break?

A: Color-ado.

Q: Why did _____
(friend's name)
cry when the cola ran out?

A: Because it was soda-pressing.

Rob Elliott

Q: How did the farmer feel when his _____ wouldn't grow?
(type of fruit)

A: Melon-choly.

Q: What did the _____
(type of candy)

say to the _____?
(different type of candy)

A: "Let's stick together."

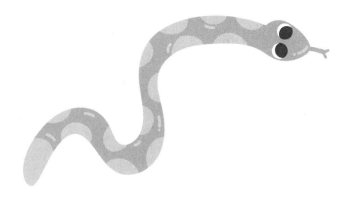